MW01135037

TO ORDER MORE:
rcwnsiiz@hotmail.com
Subject title for e-mail:
Be Wee With Bea
ENJOY reading this book

Be Wee with Bea

*Discover many rigorous exercises
to help you figure out how to deal with
just about any problem*

Liz ONeill

iUniverse

BE WEE WITH BEA

This is a work of fiction. All of the characters, names, incidents,
organizations, and dialogue in this novel are either the products
of the author's imagination or are used fictitiously.

iUniverse books may be ordered through booksellers or by contacting:

iUniverse
1663 Liberty Drive
Bloomington, IN 47403
www.iuniverse.com
1-800-Authors (1-800-288-4677)

ISBN: 978-1-5320-3062-8 (sc)
ISBN: 978-1-5320-3061-1 (e)

Print information available on the last page.

iUniverse rev. date: 08/17/2017

Contents

ACKNOWLEDGEMENT

For nearly 20 years, I taught Creative Writing in grades 6-8. I greatly envied the luxuary of writing time my students had. Many of them demonstrated exceptional skill in their compositions. An untold number of them have gone on to become writers; some already published. Some are playwrights or song composers with published recordings. Some have successfully done choreographing entertaining scenerios or stirring sermons to deliver.

I want to thank all of the hundreds of writing students, whose magnificent works have crossed my teacher's desk, for your inspiration.

Hopefully, the teacher has at least matched the student.

ABOUT THE AUTHOR

Liz K. O'Neill, a third generation Vermonter, spent 28 years in a Religious Community and has a Masters in Education with a Minor in Language Arts. She taught Writing and Literature in grades 6-8 for 20 years. She has written curricula for her undergraduate and graduate courses in her local college, where she taught for seven years.

At that same time, she volunteered and was later employed for approximately 30 years in a woman's advocacy shelter, where she developed an extensive educational website called Imbalance in Relationships and is, at the time of this writing, a Mental Health Worker in a psychiatric / substance abuse treatment program. She is very interested in archaeology,

She is currently working on another book called A Particular Friendship, which is about a woman named Beatrice. This book will cover her time before entering the Convent, during her time there, and her life after she has left the Convent.

DEDICATION

I will be ever grateful to Timothy Fisher who inspired the character of Timothy, the woodcarving, clay pot making, furniture building beaver. Timothy Fisher is an excellent, very skilled wood carver who often exhibits his works in the Middlebury, VT area. Tim who is also a proficient writer encouraged me to begin writing in one of my favorite genres, the allegory.

Finally, nearly 20 years later, I have completed his suggestion.

A NOTE TO THE READER

WARNINGS

Are signaled for the reader

By five beaver tail slaps sounded on the water

Reading this book may cause, in no particular order, the following side effects:

1. You may feel compelled to do some or all of the "Bea Wee with Bea" exercise program
2. You may discover yourself dancing in the wind
3. You may feel drawn to explore different paths than you have ever traveled
4. You may find yourself STROLLING more often than you ever have
5. You may notice that you are losing your appetite for getting into others' business
6. You may find yourself seeking different bodies of water; be they waterfalls, streams, oceans, ponds, lakes or even puddles
7. You may surprise yourself when you find yourself having a sense of humor about your actions or situations
8. You may find yourself being much better able to deal with just about any problem

INTRODUCTION

Be Wee With Bea incorporates, without being too obvious, just about every well-known recovery issue. This simply written, book contains both humor and poignancy, operating on a dual level in which both children and adults may gain insight and enjoyment. The main character, Bea the Wee Bear, could easily be any of our own biographical figure.

Much of what she experiences, many of us have experienced. She is a bit of an overeater and a severe sugar addict, who binges on exercise while bingeing on honey, her "be good to myself" treat. Her mother confused nurturing with food. She discovers ways to solve many of her problems with several exercises, one being meditation, which she calls her "Brain Exercise".

Some of the problems she deals with are: being picked on by the little bears in the neighborhood, rescuing an abused cat, an abused puppy, understanding loneliness, and working on honesty in friendships and how not to try to control everything. She has a co-dependent relationship with Scruffles the Raccoon Cat and a homeless puppy. He keeps getting bitten and beaten up by two cat gang members called Orion and Sam. Scruffles and Puppy both had poor self esteem because of abuse and neglect, as a result of living in an abusive household. Bea chose her own name when her mother wrote out "BEAR" and she dropped a drip of honey on the "R." She encouraged Scruffles to change his name from Scruffy to Scruffles.

Bea does have a very healthy friendship with Timothy the Talented Beaver, a wonderful wood carver, furnishing Bea with many nice pieces of furniture and some clay pots in which to store her honey.

So you see, my book Be Wee With Bea is quite well rounded. I hope I have piqued your interest and you will read on further.

PREFACE

Timothy, the wood carving, clay pot making, furniture building beaver, who you will meet later, introduced me to Bea the wee bear. I was immediately attracted to her. I felt energized as I joined her in her STROLLING exercise along BEA'S GOLDEN PATH. I met her dear handsome friend Scruffles the Raccoon Cat and Sweet Puppy who are the center of many of Bea's adventures; especially when she learns new things about herself.

I have learned new things about myself from using her suggestion of doing BRAIN exercises to find answers to problems. She didn't even seem to mind that I tracked mud into her home which was an enormous cave with a variety of tunnels branching out in different directions, forming very comfortable rooms. I thoroughly enjoyed watching her do her rigorous exercise program of STEPSTOOLING, FINE MOTOR WEIGHT LIFTING, TOE TOUCHING, and FLOOR TOUCHING. I laughed as she did RUNNING IN PLACE, all to be wee.

Wishing to Be Wee

Bea frequently had to fight off her bad memories and she had a lot of them. All her wee life she'd struggled with feeling she needed to work very hard to be wee. It all stemmed from when she was very little and the little mean bears who lived in the forest by her and her mom's cave would BULLY her about her size.

.

She knows in her deepest part that she is and has always been is a good wee bear. Her mom had told her that over and over many, many times; but still it was hard not to remember the voices which stuck like honey, of those mean little bears yelling and yelling. She said she thought if she did enough rigorous exercises often enough, it would make the voices go away. Her friends accepted her just the way she was. After doing her exercises for so many summers, Bea began to NOTICE that she didn't do her vigorous exercises for the same reasons anymore. She somehow knew her exercises were helping her in other ways to solve her problems.

When I asked how she got the name Bea, which seemed an unusual name for a wee bear, she explained that it is the name she has carried since the day she learned how to write. She had, during many of her STROLLING exercises with her mom, seen names of things written on signs and had wondered what her name would look like.

She asked her mom to write her name on a piece of paper so she could learn how to write it. Well, she was having a little honey -- later to be known as her "be good to myself" treat and dropped a drip of it right on the "R" at the end of her name. So, licking her yummy right paw and gripping with all of her might, a purple crayon in her left, she copied the letters one after another, B-E-A. You see, her mom hadn't ever quite decided what to name her so she had always called her Bear. Her mom was so pleased to see that Bea had chosen her own name. She was already beginning her exercises of solving problems.

She told me that when her mom called outside for her, there was sometimes a bit of confusion, because the wrong bee would come. Bea's eyes glimmered as she told me that she really, really didn't mind. She liked bees because they were the ones who made her "be good to myself" treat. Bea told me that sometimes, even though she knew that her mom loved her, Bea had felt like giving up when the little bears yelled "No Fat Bears" every time she came around to play. She was sure if she were wee, maybe they would have invited her to play. She decided that she just wouldn't eat anymore.

Every time her mom asked her if she wanted any honey, she said that she wasn't hungry, no matter how much her stomach rumbled, grumbled or growled. Why should she have a "be good to myself" treat when she did not feel good about herself? After so many mean bears had said bad things to her and about her, for so many times, for so long, Bea had begun to believe them. She had stopped drawing on paper and wrote all over her fur with different colored crayons. She believed those little bears must be right because how could that many of them be wrong. It must be true. She never counted how many there were but it felt like a lot. It had always been a very painful blurr in her memory.

She always had hoped that she could become invisible so the mean bears wouldn't know she was around. But then there were times when she didn't want to be invisible; but she was. Maybe she'd wished too hard and things got out of balance. Being invisible turned out to be as painful as being visible. When she was invisible no one seemed to see how sad she was or how she was being treated. She would go somewhere else in her head. Maybe her thoughts could do some kind of magic and make her a good wee bear instead of a BAD FAT BEAR. She wanted to tell her mom how horrible she felt inside, but didn't know how to start. Her mom saw how very sad and hurt Bea was and told Bea she did not have to be mean to herself because others were cruel to her. Bea was so surprised that her mom knew some of what was going on without having to say a word. It made it easier. She still didn't say anything.

Reassuring her with a great big bear hug, that she was a GOOD WEE BEAR, her mom told her it was time for her to learn to talk to the MAKER who passes onto us all the wisdom we need. She taught her how to both talk and listen to the MAKER OF WEE BEARS. When Bea told the MAKER OF WEE BEARS how hard she was wishing to be wee, she heard an idea of how to be wee and still enjoy her "be good to myself" treat -- a rigorous exercise program. This was the first of Bea's many wonderful BRAIN exercises. A very satisfied wee bear, she decided to call it "Be Wee With Bea".

The "Be Wee With Bea" rigorous exercise program will cost you nothing. She uses things found right in her home. You can too. She didn't need to go out and buy an expensive exercise machine. She gets the same kind of exercise going up and down her stepstool to get her pots of honey that are up high on shelves, which requires stretching the ribs. This might even prevent Bea from shrinking as they say people do. The part that makes this a rigorous exercise is she doesn't do this just a few times or for just a few minutes; she carries on this activity many, many times all day long and sometimes into the wee hours of the night.

She is so dedicated that often she wakes up and realizes that she hasn't done her STOOLSTEPPING for a while. She gets right up without hesitation or reluctance. This exercise also has an added bonus that the store- bought exercise machine doesn't. She is also doing fairly heavy WEIGHT LIFTING as the pots are brimming full as she lifts and carries them slowly down her steps. The weights being lifted as she does the going down part, are of course heavier than they are for the going up part on the STOOLSTEPPER. This graduated weight program may be a bit backwards. Usually the weights are increased rather than decreased as the program progresses; but Bea knows it will have good effects on her confidence and self-esteem anyway. She realizes that her tummy has a bit of a full feeling so it probably is just as well that the honey pots are empty and don't weigh very much. Her strength might decrease as her tummy gets fuller.

Once, she got so excited about this exercise program that while she was rushing her FINE MOTOR WEIGHT LIFTING -- which simply means having a big pawful of her "be good to myself" treat, she dropped a drip on her toes. That was when she discovered another exercise which she calls TOE TOUCHING, which of course balances out the full tummy and a bending exercise. Another similar exercise, but one which calls for a wee more stretching, is FLOOR TOUCHING. Sometimes FLOOR TOUCHING can develop into RUNNING IN PLACE, if the weights get too tippy and fall on the floor and her feet get all stuck up in this exercise. She may try to use her paw to clean off the honey covering her feet, but if this does not work right off she will use it an opportunity for her to do some of her DANCE exercises.

The Dance

Bea absolutely loves to dance. She dances when she's happy, sad, when she does her TALK exercise, along with her STROLLING exercise, when she is trying to figure out a problem and even during her rigorous exercise program. Someone might ask where the music is? Wondering how anyone could dance without music. Bea finds music everywhere; especially when she's near the water. She hears the rocks and stones rolling over each other making a sweet tinkling sound. She hears them singing their stories of the journey they've been on for hundreds and hundreds of years. Rolling, smoothing their sharp edges; they teach Bea about the struggles in her life. Solving her problems one at a time, she will smooth out and become calmer appreciating everything around her. This will lead her to her THANKING THE MAKER OF EVERYTHING.

She loves to listen to the water sing. Doing her NOTICE exercise helps her be able to hear that the singing is different almost every day and in different kinds of water. There is a drumming sound when the water is falling from up high. She does a different dance here, drumming with her feet. She does a swishing dance when the water makes swishing sounds. In areas where the water is very still, she just stands there quietly swaying back and forth and doing her SIMPLY ENJOYING HER LIFE exercise.

The water, no matter where it is or how it is flowing, sings a special song to Bea about solving her problems. Doing her NOTICE exercise she can see that the water goes around and over the rocks. A lot of the sparkling, glistening, sun-reflecting water just goes around the rocks. It adjusts to the obstacles in front of it. Bea always wants to do this; but finds it difficult; which is why she does her BRAIN exercise so often.

She realized at that moment, she kind of acts like a BULLY with her problems. She supposed that sometimes that was a good exercise; but maybe not always. Maybe she could learn to bend like water. That was it. Wasn't it ? The water kind of bends around the rocks and stuck logs. It definitely needs to bend around the logs in Timothy's Dam he worked so hard on for days and days.

She began to do her BRAIN exercise right then. She wondered how her friends really felt when she was trying to force a problem to come out the way SHE THOUGHT IT SHOULD -- not the way the MAKER knew would be best. When she was putting her nose in the wrong place, it usually ended up being a sorry nose and she would find herself and her nose just plain STUCK. She just had to learn to move on from her PLANNING and SCANNING. Others and their problems, all too often seemed like just another exercise for her. Something to take her away from her bad memories and bad feeling about herself. She knew she had to begin to be serious about doing her DETACHMENT FROM THINGS WHICH HAVE A HOLD ON YOU exercise.

She kind of knew how upset, hurt and DISCOURAGED Timothy would be if the water acted like a BULLY and pushed all of his logs out of the way and rushed through everything he had worked on. The beautiful strong TIMOTHY's DAM would be DEMOLISHED even before he'd had time to finish it. Bea thought, maybe, she was pushing through her friends' exercise of working on solving their

7

problem before they even finished. Maybe, she should wait until they asked for help from her. But what if they never asked? Then what would she do ? That would be very hard. She was so used to rushing in to help her mom with every little thing. Because her father was never around, someone had to help. Remembering back, she realized, her mom was trying to tell her she needed to figure her problem out without Bea sticking her nose into everything. Her mom never said it that way; but Bea now understood. But this was a longtime exercise for Bea. This was another lesson she could learn from the song the water sang.

The water teaches Bea how to be safe too. Sometimes when the water is acting like the little bears that were mean to her when they would BULLY her, the rough waters sang of DANGER. Just as she stayed away from them, Bea stays away from that kind of water which sings a song to remind her to take care of herself.

Bea, the swirling bear, can be seen spinning with her arms spread out as far as they can be, when she listens to the breeze going through the trees. She doesn't know for sure if it is the wind singing or the leaves but she loves how it makes her feel. Just as with the water, it is different everyday and sometimes from moment to moment. Bea felt a bit of a TWINGE as she had a bad memory of what happened when she was little and the wind barely had time to sing of DANGER to her mom and the large elm tree came crashing down on their cave, gouging a very large hole in their home. She still practiced her ON ALERT exercise when the wind began to change its song to a faster deeper whistling sound. If that all too familiar song continued for too long, and she could feel her FEARS growing with the strength of the BULLY-like wind, Bea did her SPRINTING exercise and got out of there as fast as she could.

Oh, but the birds, yes the birds. What beautiful songs they sing. When Bea does her NOTICE exercise, she hears so many different sounds. Some even seem to be dancing on the thin branches, causing the branches with leaves and pine bows to dance also. Bea can't help but join them with her DANCE exercise.

Sometimes the song the wind, leaves, water or birds sang, matched how Bea was feeling. The woeful moaning song helped her do her NOTICE exercise. She never wanted to burden her friends with her SADNESS or ANGER. She preferred to be still like the calm water. She didn't feel so alone with her feelings of loss when she heard the mourning dove or the wind sing the song that was in her heart as she thought of her wonderful time with Timothy and how much she missed her mom. She also missed the happy times at play that she felt the mean little bears took away from her, not allowing her to play with them.

She often wondered in her BRAIN exercise what things would have been like if her father had been around more and if she could really have had the COURAGE to tell her mom what those mean little bears were doing to her and how they were treating her. She realized that was one of the main reasons she started to PRETEND. She didn't really want to have to pretend, but it seemed the only way she knew. She had to PRETEND that she didn't really mind that her father was never there. She didn't want to hurt her mom's feelings. She needed to take care of her.

She wondered if she'd learned to PRETEND from her mom, who never said a bad word about the fact that her father was so absent. When Bea would do her NOTICE exercise she could see great sadness in her mom's loving eyes. Maybe that was one of her mom's exercises; which had become her own too. But her mom did a good job at pretending. She taught Bea how to take care of others' feelings by not letting them know how you really feel. Mom still laughed and played with Bea and had her join in her DANCE exercise and her STROLLING exercise everyday. She even showed Bea all of the good paths where all of the best berries were and even an occasional pile of nuts saved by the squirrels, when no one was at home. She pointed out her favorite streams to catch fish.

But, the best of course, the places to get honey. Her mom warned her though, if she stuck her nose into the yummiest of places, she must be ready to get her nose stung atleastonce and sometimes many times. But to Bea, it sounded very worth it. That exercise, as you have heard, has taught her many lessons over the years.

Every once in awhile, some angry memories would sneak in. Bea knew it was time for her to go stand at the edge of the swirling, frothy waters. It was a mystery to Bea, why this makes her feel so calm; but it does. She suspects it has something to do with THE MAKER.

So, Bea does have music when she dances. It is all of these songs she carries in her heart.

No One Caring

On one of her rigorous STROLLING exercises Bea the wee bear met up with a very unkempt looking cat who introduced himself as Scruffy. That name certainly suited him as his fur was all matted and stuck up with some sort of goo. He explained that his owners had children who were never told by their mom to wash their hands or face. And whenever they touched him or nuzzled their faces into his fur they left clumps of something sticky on him, like lollipops or ice-cream. He had given up on trying to stay clean. Even though cats were supposed to have very strong tongues, his got very tired and very, very sticky. When Bea did her NOTICE exercise, she could see how Scruffy's ribs showed through his sad looking, clumped up, matted hair.

She thought to herself that she would not have to ever worry that her ribs were showing. Then she caught herself and realized she was talking negative about herself like those mean bears did. She did not want to do that anymore. She brought her attention back to when Scruffy was saying that his favorite food had become the pizza crust. When Bea looked puzzled he continued to explain how it was the food left from what the kids dropped on the floor under the table. He found himself hanging out a lot down there. He had to be careful not to also bite into some strange object or moldy food stuck to the floor when he was gobbling up the good stuff. He ate WHEN the kids ate, which didn't seem to be very often. So he spent a lot of time going around door to door and from garbage can to garbage can.

He told Bea that his owners had many, many problems. The kids' dad drank a lot of something in a lot of bottles and a lot of cans. This made him change quickly from fun to very scary; an unsafe place for Scruffy to be around. The angry man would kick at poor Scruffy; one time he almost kicked Scruffy down the long steep set of stairs. He had had some practice flying; the little girl used to fling poor Scruffy down the stairs almost daily. But to be kicked down them was another thing altogether. Scruffy knew this was what the very sad little girl must have thought would help and found some fun in throwing him down the stairs and watching him fly. He could put up with that; after all cats can land on their feet and be kind of OK. But this man who teetered around and bumped into things and threw pizza boxes was too much for Scruffy. Bea asked him where the mom was during all of this and Scruffy said that she was rushing around trying to get the kids out of the way and trying to calm the man down. She didn't have much time for the kids because she was busy worrying about whether the man was going to drink another can of that bad stuff. She cried a lot and just sat around watching TV. The kids would say they were hungry or needed something and she acted as if she couldn't hear them.

Scruffy said he hoped he was a comfort to them as they petted him with their dirty sticky hands and hugged and nuzzled his soft hair with their gooey, smudged faces. He said he felt so conflicted. He knew he should stay there for them but he couldn't take it anymore and needed to take care of himself. He did miss them already and hoped they would be able to find their way through life. But he had to be out of there. Bea was quickly doing her BRAIN exercise, knowing this a time to learn something about her way of living. She could never hear ideas about taking care of herself, enough. She sometimes had this same problem. She told Scruffles about her DETACHMENT FROM THINGS WHICH HAVE A HOLD ON YOU exercise. He said he would do that exercise and was hoping they would meet again; he thought he could learn a lot from Bea.

Sharing With Others

Bea the wee Bear realized that this problem was bigger than she. But she was determined to help her new friend find his HOPE. He was scared and lonely and she knew that she could not leave him in this terrible situation. She put all thoughts of her rigorous STROLLING exercise aside and moved a distance away from Scruffy to begin her BRAIN exercise -- which simply meant a very rigorous thinking time, away from distractions while she worked on figuring out an answer to a problem. She knew if she chose to invite him to be a guest in her home there would be difficult times, but they could take it one step at a time. She did, however, quickly take a mental inventory of her supply of honey -- did she have enough to share?

When the answer came up "yes," she invited Scruffy to live with her. He had no reason to go back, so he accepted her invitation. Bea, this wee kind bear, told Scruffy that his dish would never be empty again. She did her best to help him get some of the snarls out and to clean him up a bit. She knew that after living by herself for so long, she needed to watch her FEARS, which at times like these, snuck in-- fears that she wouldn't have enough of everything to be able to share, especially her "be good to myself" treat. When she finally did her NOTICE exercise, she realized that Scruffy didn't even want to take all of her honey; he didn't even like honey. Still, she found herself doing her ON GUARD exercise.

This was her old way of dealing with the FEARS she used to get when she had to share everything with her brother and sister. When they would begin arguing over who got the most, her mom would tell them they would have to measure or count everything out evenly. But now, her mom wasn't around to help; she had died a few years earlier. Bea hadn't felt this way in a long time and didn't like it very much. She knew it was time to do the BRAIN exercise her mom had taught her.

She remembered that THE MAKER OF THE BEES had taken care of things in the past. She quieted herself the way her mom had shown her and began her talk to the MAKER OF THE BEES, telling of her FEARS. At first she felt a BUZZING, as if fifty bees were flying around inside her. Then after a few quiet minutes, she heard a nice comforting hum in the air, of busy bees making honey and she knew things would work out for both her and Scruffy. But, we all know that sharing does not always go smoothly. As you might have guessed, Bea was doing a little bit of her PRETEND exercise in her mind of IMAGINATION. And her IMAGINATION was very strong. As strong as the DAM in TIMOTHY'S POND. It was not until reality hit her square in the face that she had to search for COURAGE to be honest with herself. At first Scruffy was content to hang out in the cave because as promised, after accompanying Bea to the nearby babbling brook to catch fish, he had more than he could eat. His tummy was not used to so much and so rich a meal. EVER.

Bea would have done well to do her NOTICE exercise and listen to the song the brook was singing. If she had; she would have heard the message of CHAOS and CONFUSION. But, she was busy thinking of how happy she was making Scruffy. The first night ever, that Scruffy had been able to just RELAX and ENJOY HIS LIFE, he couldn't. He was so restless. Bea of course was tired and wanted PEACE and QUIET. She was just not used to this. She was rudely awakened when she heard the strangest sound she'd ever heard. It grated terribly on her ears and her nerves. It seemed to be coming from right beside her.

It was! Scruffy was yowling not meowing in the sweet way when they first met. Not the contented purring she found to be so rewarding for her labors, when he was enjoying the fish that Bea had caught for him. NO. It was a very loud and annoying YOWL. Bea could have none of this. She promptly scooped him up much like her mom had in her frenzy to get them to safety. But this was for an entirely different purpose. Bea needed to SLEEP. She did a quick BRAIN exercise; clearly not thorough enough of an exercise as we will soon see. After setting Scruffy down in a farback room, returned to her still warm leaf & grass comfortable bedding. That solution brought far worse results. Just as the lightning flash during storms illuminated every wall in the cave, the cat YOWLING was bouncing off, reverberating from every room in the entire cave.

Bea could stand it no more. He had to GO. She stormed to the back of the cave, into the room that was the loudest and swiped Scruffy between her very angry paws; thankfully, no claws used, and proceed to remove him from the home Bea so generously offered him. It could be called an evening eviction. She set him down, in not such a gentle manner, and said nothing more. Actually, if she had taken time to do her NOTICE exercise, she would have realized that she'd spoken not a word that entire time, nor had she remembered to breathe throughout that whole incident. She then without much delay, was able to return to the spot a wee bear USUALLY can easily fall asleep and she instantly did without even having any of her "be good to myself" treat, which we certainly might expect.

As she was preparing to do her talk to THE MAKER exercise as she did to begin every bear day, she had a bad memory, not of when she was young, but about last night. She had to do her BRAIN exercise to understand what happened last night. What had she done? Then it hit her, what had gone on. And it hit her even harder after she did her HUMBLE exercise when she remembered how she had acted. Poor Scruffy, she had acted like a BULLY toward him. She was no better than the mean little bears or the people he had lived with. How must he feel? She knew how she felt. HORRIBLE. She had to find him.

There was no time for her "Be Wee With Bea" rigorous exercise program on the STOOLSTEPPER, no WEIGHT LIFTING, graduated or otherwise, no need for FINE MOTOR WEIGHT LIFTING, TOE TOUCHING or even FLOOR TOUCHING. She felt so STUCK now as if she were RUNNING IN PLACE, going nowhere. She just couldn't seem to progress. It was a very different kind of STUCK. She had to find him. She SPRINTED from room to room of the cave. Even with all her FEARS growing and with the fifty bees buzzing around inside her, she was able to do a NOTICE exercise. For the first time, at that moment, she realized how very, very vast her cave was, or at least, it certainly seemed very expansive right now. He was nowhere to be found. Where could he have disappeared to? Was she so much worse than his family, that he would prefer to go back to sitting under the table on the dirty floor, waiting for a piece of pizza crust to drop from the children's grubby hands. She decided she'd start doing her INVESTIGATION exercise looking for him on all the paths that would be familiar for him. Ah, the first might be where she's met him. She SPRINTED to that now very empty spot and down to the brook where they had gone earlier yesterday to catch fish for Scruffy.

You will later learn about why she would want to stop to visit Willow and who Willow was. But for now, it is enough to know that Bea had a wonderful friend who would always be there with undivided attention for her. At this point, she felt like thrashing and crying; Willow had always helped many feel better by just listening. And Bea was absolutely certain Willow would be able to help. For some reason, just knowing she'd be there for Bea, helped her to do her REMAIN CALM exercise, an exercise she knew she should have used last night. She decided that she could wait to see Willow and stop to see if Timothy was anywhere to be found. If not, then she'd go to see Willow. She was closer to where he was. Even though she hadn't eaten and her tummy was probably quite empty, she did her SPRINTING exercise hoping to hear the reassuring slap sounded on the water. To their agreement, she would slap the water two times so he would know it was her and not some predator. And he'd answer with one slap. As she came nearer TIMOTHY'S POND, her FEARS started growing. What if Timothy wasn't in his lodge. She stood there with her "if only's" and "why's" and "no it can't be's". Then she made her COURAGE get bigger than her FEARS and sounded two loud slaps on the water. She was WAITING and WAITING. Had she done her NOTICE exercise, she would have realized that it had been a long time since she had taken a breath. Terrible SILENCE. No sound of water being slapped by a Timothy the Beaver.

Finally. Always finally. When all else fails, Bea remembers to do her talk to THE MAKER of EVERYTHING. Beavers, Cats, and best of all wee bears. When she heard the gentle slapping on water sound, she knew somehow things would work out. This and the buzzing of bees always reassured

Bea. It felt safer for her to wait in the silence and WAIT and be CALM without trying to force a problem to come out the way SHE THOUGHT IT SHOULD -- not the way the MAKER knew would be best.

Then she heard a Timothy the Beaver's tail slap sounded one time on the water. She sounded two slaps and there was Timothy swimming right to the edge of the POND. She was so relieved. Surely he'd know what she could do. At first she was hesitant to tell him the whole story and how she had acted. But then she remembered how understanding he was about so many of her limitations. So she told him everything that had happened and was as HONEST as she could be about how she had reacted and didn't even blame Scruffy for her behavior. Even though it was hard not to give him a little blame; she didn't. Then she sadly mumbled that she wasn't sure she DESERVED to have a friend like Scruffy.

Timothy told her that she did DESERVE to have such a friend as Scruffy. He offered some good SUGGESTIONS about what she could do. They made a lot of sense to Bea; but she was pretty sure it would mean a lot of work on her part. She had to be ready to do more hard work, but she knew that THE MAKER would always be there to help. If she would leave Scruffy's bowl full of fish outside the cave and wait for him, he would come back because he knows Bea cares for him. But that was easy. The hardest part would be that she needed to be HUMBLE and let Scruffy say what he wanted. When Timothy asked Bea if she had asked Scruffy what he wanted; she had to admit to him that she hadn't EVEN thought of doing that.

Bea was hoping Timothy could save her that painful part. But he said he did not know what Scruffy would want, only Scruffy could answer that question. She thanked him very much for helping and remembered to ask him how he was doing. He said he was doing very well. They said a good bye to each other and Bea was on her way to follow Timothy's SUGGESTIONS.

Bea stopped by the favorite fishing spot to get lots of fish for Scruffy's bowl to be set outside. She placed his yummy smelling bowl at the mouth of the cave, then poised herself in a GET READY spot. She was practicing her ALERT but CALM exercise. More WAITING. It seemed lately all she did was WAIT. It did seem like a such SENSELESS exercise, but she knew it was necessary as was all WAITINGS if the desired results were deemed worthwhile enough and Bea felt very strongly that this was worth it. It was growing darker and Bea was losing HOPE. Doing her talk to the MAKER OF HOPE made WAITING tolerable.

There was no buzzing of bees or gentle slap on the water that came next. Only a scraping sound of a Scruffy cat moving the bowl of fish as he ravenously ate. This was Bea's maybe ONLY chance. Instead of Scruffy SPRINGING, it was Bea as she skittered Scruffy and his bowl into the cave. As she did this, in the same breath, she spouted out that she was WRONG. So WRONG the way she had treated him and she wanted to start over if he would have it that way.

During their discussion, which was very brief, Scruffy said that he needed more freedom. He was not used to being in any one place for very long. He slept with each of the children on their sheetless mattresses. He couldn't stay long with the youngest because his diaper smelled too awful, even for a garbage rummaging scruffy raccoon cat. He admitted he could, eventually, get very used to this way of life. It was just going to take some time. And that Bea needed to give him that time.

Caring About Others

Scruffy began to eat better. In addition to retrieving honey from bees' hives, bears are good at catching fish. Scruffy finally dared to tell Bea that he would much rather have fish than honey, or some old hard piece of pizza crust. He began to look a lot better too. And as time went on he began to feel a lot better about himself. During one of her BRAIN exercises, Bea thought about how the name Scruffy made her feel. It reminded her of that scruffy, scrawny cat she had met on one of her rigorous STROLLING exercises. He was nowhere to be found. In his place was a handsome raccoon cat who had the most beautiful fur and a flowing tail which looked like the mane of some of her horse friends. It was time for him to change his name. She thought of a name that would be much more dignified -- Scruffles the Raccoon Cat. It was set; from now on, he would be known as Scruffles the Raccoon Cat.

Just because Scruffles felt better it did not, unfortunately, mean that everything around him got better. Sometimes Bea would hear him crying in his sleep and watch his little legs beating back and forth as if he were trying to get away from something. His bad memories had come back ever since the two meanest cats you could ever meet began showing up. Orian, an ugly orange tomcat, outweighed Scruffles by at least eight pounds. Scruffles had put on some weight by now but he still weighed only twelve pounds. She was afraid he was no match against such a massive cat. Scruffles did surprise her, though.

After a terrible battle, finding only ONE clump of Scruffles' fur on the ground, she counted THREE blond clumps of Orian's hair from his strong broad back.

From then on, Orian didn't seem as interested in fighting Scruffles. He went back to fighting squirrels where he had much more success. The more terrible of the two was Sam, who didn't seem to fear anything. His teeth were so very, very sharp and could dig deep into Scruffles' back and tail. By now Scruffles' bad memories were back most of the time, even when he wasn't napping. Whenever he saw Sam, poor Scruffles just froze. Bea knew that her friend could not handle things on his own and that she needed to do a rigorous BRAIN exercise.

Rescuing Others

Bea remembered why Bears are able to catch fish; they like to splash in water. She did not remember ever seeing any cat splashing in water, as much as they love the "be good to themselves" treat -- fish. She knew what she would do. Every time that mean cat came by to bother Scruffles she would throw a pot of -- certainly not honey -- but water, on him. With excitement and hopes that her plan would work, she gathered her empty honey pots, filled them with water, and placed them in a GET READY spot. Every time Scruffles was sunning himself, she would stand by, doing her ON GUARD exercise, holding her wee bear breath, watching and waiting for Sam to show his sinister Siamese self. After several minutes had passed and no Sam, Bea realized she hadn't taken a breath and that she needed to remember to be ALERT but RELAXED. She was ready with a filled pot when a slinking shadow caught her cautious eye. She splashed him full force with the first of many pots lined up in a row. Boy, did he tear out of there. She thought that was the end of it, surely. Now she could really relax.

She couldn't believe her wee bear eyes, which got very big, when she saw the stunned or just stubborn Siamese standing right over Scruffles. This time, her throw got Scruffles a little wet, but sent that rambunctious cat back under his porch. Bea later found out that Scruffles loved water. He was not afraid to stand over a slightly frozen puddle and attempt to crack it open to get to the water. He would be so focused on this exercise that he didn't seem to care if he became covered with about a half an inch of snow.

Bea, now a little skeptical at the results of a cat being splashed with water, needed to make sure that Sam was back where he belonged. When she found him lying so innocently at rest, she felt reassured and headed back to enjoy the sun with Scruffles. It didn't take long for her to discover a new exercise, not rigorous STROLLING, but very rigorous RUNNING FOR YOUR LIFE. She felt a hot little breath on the back of her legs. Ever so slowly peeking around, she saw Sam about to nip at her wee bear heels with those sharp pointy teeth of his. Swiftly skittering to safety, she began to do her BRAIN exercise. Once again she had come upon a problem too big for her to handle alone.

The Answer

Sometimes, the answer to a problem came to Bea by recalling what had worked in the past. This situation reminded her of the time when there was no honey to be found. The bees just didn't seem to be making it fast enough for her needs. She knew she certainly couldn't make the honey herself, as much as she'd like to be able to. She had that same desperate feeling now; no matter how hard she tried, she just couldn't make things work out right. In times passed, she had done her TALK TO THE MAKER exercise, THE MAKER OF THE BEES. She figured the ONE WHO MADE THE BEES could get the bees to make more honey, so she could be sure she always had enough of her "be good to myself" treat. When she did her LISTEN TO THE MAKER exercise, she heard a peaceful reassuring buzzing in the air and knew that the MAKER OF THE BEES had heard her request. She decided she'd take a risk and ask the MAKER OF THE BEES about this problem. After all, the MAKER OF THE BEES was also the MAKER OF CATS. As she did her LISTEN TO THE MAKER exercise, there was a stillness in the air, which told her to be still. She knew that somehow things would work themselves out, without her help.

A very pleasant peaceful week had passed, before she realized that she had not seen any sign of Sam. She knew he would not return. She did not know where he had gone, but did not question the ways of the MAKER OF THE BEES, the MAKER OF CATS, and best of all the MAKER OF WEE BEARS.

Often while basking in the warm sun as cats love to do, Scruffles would tell Bea how wonderful his life with her was and how safe and happy he felt now. Listening to Scruffles talk about his sad times started Bea remembering what it was like when she was little. Her father was away a lot gathering honey. He seemed to have to travel further and further each time. She had to share everything with her younger brother and sister. They didn't seem to get picked on as much as Bea, by the other little bears. Then again, they didn't love honey as much either. They seemed satisfied to eat fish. That just would not do for Bea; she had to have her honey.

Sometimes, Bea's little tummy was quite full of honey and it kind of showed. She thought the honey must have moved down into her legs because they looked kind of full too. The other bears must have wished they could have as much honey to eat as she did; or they were jealous because they didn't have a mom who loved them so much that she would make sure there was lots and lots of honey for them anytime they wanted it and who did things to help them feel better when they were sad.

They were very, very mean to her. They called her FAT BEAR. She didn't understand what these words really meant, but from the way they growled and hissed and wrinkled up their noses, she knew it must be very bad. She felt awful. But she knew that even though they were not good to her, her mom was; she gave her honey to help her feel better. This was the beginning of her "be good to myself" treat; which meant that every time Bea had a problem to figure out, was having a difficult time, was sad, frustrated, angry, tired, disappointed or her FEARS were growing or even when she was feeling happy, she would have at least one pawful of honey. And usually this required more than just one lonely pawful. But it truly was a great answer to any problem.

The Dirt Path

Now you will hear the whole wonderful story of how Bea met Willow. One of her rigorous STROLLING exercises brought Bea to a new area she'd never visited before. Only small patches of the blue sky could be seen through the many very tall pine trees surrounding her. The ground was so velvety soft to the touch of the rough pads on her weary feet. As she kept walking in the direction she believed would take her home, the ground changed from pine needles to soft dirt. She sensed a coolness as her hot feet sank into the dirt that was the color of golden honey. This, as you might imagine, reminded her that a long journey had passed since she had done any of her FINE MOTOR WEIGHT LIFTING. Much to the relief of her wee bear tummy, the path brought her out very near her home. After doing a little STEPSTOOLING, followed by FINE MOTOR WEIGHT LIFTING, and lastly one TOE TOUCH, she decided to return to her new find.

She loved the adventure of going into untread territory and actually finding her way back home. To get back to that lovely pine forest, she decided to take her new shortcut, the dirt path. She stopped short when she saw that the path had footprints on it. Could some other creature have discovered this pathway too? The prints looked to be that of a wee bear going toward Bea's home. She did not remember seeing any such creature. Trying her feet for size in the prints, she realized they were her very own wee bear prints. She was excited to think that her prints were still there even after she had left the path.

She made some more impressions in the soft dirt. Then walked off the path a distance and quickly returned to see if her prints were still there. They were.

She felt so proud to imagine others, traveling along this path, coming upon her prints, and knowing they were the famous footprints of Bea the wee bear. She didn't know if this path had a name; but in her gleeful wee bear heart, she changed it to BEA'S GOLDEN PATH. This brought her so much happiness; she returned time and time again. Sometimes, she found lots of jumbled markings from other creatures, who had finally happened upon her discovery. Other times, the playful whistling wind had erased them. This did not discourage Bea; she would just keep coming back.

Bea just loved traveling along BEA'S GOLDEN PATH and went that way many days a week. But, on one of her STROLLING exercises Bea felt drawn to go on an even newer path where she saw a possible friend off in the distance. Bea's mom taught her there are always possibilities; but sometimes you had to do the ON GUARD exercise and take the next step, even if the FEARS come back. And they sure could after her bad memories with those mean little bears not wanting to be friends with her. She a bit worried this might happen as she carefully tiptoed toward her new sad friend.

She began her BRAIN exercise, as she looked around and saw no one with her as she stood a bit slumped, alone. There was no furry friend like Scruffles to help her feel better. When Bea asked her why she was so sad, she told Bea that it had to do with the children who had come to visit her over the many years. Bea had to keep doing her BRAIN exercise because she could not understand why that would make her friend sad. She needed to know what to say next. She somehow knew there must be more to this and that it had something to do with FEARS. For once Bea found the gift of silence within herself to be able to let her finish.

She told Bea that she had stood in the torrential rains, powerful winds and beautiful warm sunshine waiting for them to come, some with tear smudged faces, some with old bruises covered over with new ones. She loved having the children gather around her. She was especially thrilled to hear them laughing

Bea was so glad she did let Willow continue talking without rudely interrupting. Willow. That was what Bea affectionately named her. It was important for everything to have names for Bea. She felt if something or some creature could be named, then THE MAKER would be able to sort them our more easily and be able to remember them better and could help them sooner. It also was important to Bea remember them so she could hold in her heart in a more organized way. Just as she organized her pots of honey, from full, to half full, to empty. Bea knew she was right when her tall friend began to weep and told Bea that she knew that the children hid sadness and FEARS in their deepest parts. She could see it their eyes and the ways they stood, or threw themselves at her or to the ground.

Bea wanted to ask her weeping friend questions, her usual "whys, what if's and how could this be?" But she, fortunately, remembered the manners her mom had taught her. Then she remembered that she could do her talk to The MAKER OF WILLOW TREES exercise to help her friend. As Bea moved a little to the side to do this, she noticed scars in Willow's bark. Some were very old and had healed over some look fresh. It didn't look like beaver tooth marks.

She'd seen plenty of Timothy's beautiful carved wood. She had to ask Willow. She promised herself, it would be just one little question as she was vigorously doing her BRAIN exercise. She asked Willow what had made those deep blunt marks in her tender bark. Willow told her that angry sticks held by the sad children had cut deep into her bark. Willow had to think of the sticks as being angry, because she could not handle believing any child would want to hurt her. She felt the degree of the ugliness the scars represented how ugly the child's life was. But she didn't mind any of their attacks of rage, loss and sense of desolation if it helped them feel better, not so alone and able work out some of their problems.

Bea was surprised and at the same time thrilled that Willow must know about THE MAKER too; THE MAKER OF TREES and THE MAKER OF CHILDREN. Now Bea knew things would be OK. She told Willow that she understood about the FEARS and how it felt like fifty bees were flying around inside her. She wondered if Willow felt like fifty termites were chewing in circles inside her, but of course she didn't ask. Willow said she worried that she hadn't helped the children enough. She didn't feel she gave them enough HOPE. Bea did a little dance inside her BRAIN to hear that Willow worried too. She also understood that all too familiar sinking feeling, of trying to find HOPE.

Bea once again knew she needed to do her BRAIN exercise to help her friend feel better. Here, Willow had been helping so many children for ever and now she needed help to find her own HOPE again. She asked THE MAKER OF HOPE what to say. THE MAKER told her to tell Willow that she held the memory for these children in her scars, in the music she played through her grace-filled leaves. She should tell Willow as she weeps her deep heart song she should also remember to stand tall because it is a wonderful thing she does.

Bea danced on her way back home as she heard the music THE MAKER spoke of. She felt a very warm, happy feeling and could not help but smile and thank THE MAKER. As she continued her STROLLING exercise, she made sure she remembered the special markings on this path. She had learned so much from her new friend, Willow and hoped to return to learn more.

A Strange Warning Smell

There was a strange smell in the air, which warned Bea to do her STROLLING exercise in a new area. She had a very unsettled feeling in her tummy, far worse than the feeling of fifty bees swarming. It was more like what she might be feeling if for some reason she'd eaten a whole pot of bad honey that had suddenly turned black. Tossing and twisting restlessly the whole night, with that awful smell, lurking, covering all other familiar smells; it was Bea's turn to tell her dear friend Scruffles the Raccoon Cat about her terrible dreams. She didn't fully understand what they meant but was certain they had something to do with BEA'S GOLDEN PATH. Scruffles stayed by her bedside the entire night, comforting her and telling her he would go with her in the morning to help her make new footprints if something had happened to them.

The sun did not peek over the trees soon enough for Bea. Scruffles' eyes didn't seem to want to open; he was in a very deep sleep. Bea was so anxious that she didn't even take time for her "be good to myself" treat, nor would she allow Scruffles to do his morning cat bathing. Bea, usually a very patient wee bear, was aware of her impatience with Scruffles' slow steady pace. She had a sense that something was terribly wrong, and wanted to do SPRINTING rather than her usual STROLLING exercise.

Scruffles and Bea both changed their minds about making any new footprints and just stared at the ooze which covered the path that used to be called BEA'S GOLDEN

32

PATH. It wasn't gold anymore. It was black, the blackest black they had ever seen. And sadder yet, all of Bea's footprints were buried. All of the footprints of all of the creatures who had ever been privileged to tread upon BEA'S GOLDEN PATH were somewhere here underneath two inches of blacktop.

She she told Scruffles that she was worried that someday all of the mud, topsoil, fallen pine needles, green grasses and other unnamed dirt paths would be covered with blacktop. It was definitely time to do a very rigorous BRAIN exercise. She decided to talk to the MAKER OF PINE TREES. She heard the comforting HUM of the bees making honey and somehow knew that things would work out the way the MAKER knew would be best.

When a pine cone landed in front of her, she noticed a tiny pine tree which had sprouted up through a rock ledge. She smiled as she pictured pine trees and grasses breaking through this manmade blackness and all of the traces of creatures being rediscovered, best of all, the GOLDEN part of BEA'S GOLDEN PATH.

No Good Home

One of her most rigorous STROLLING exercises that Bea the wee bear was on, had to come to a sudden halt when she saw the saddest sight she'd ever seen. Sadder than Scruffy. Sadder than Willow. Bea was wondering if she should do her INVESTIGATION exercise. She remembered it sometimes got her nose into sticky situations. She was quickly doing her SCANNING and PLANNING. Those fifty bees were flying around inside her again. The FEARS were coming back. What big ears. She looked like she was part bat but with no wings. Bea could tell this little one had been walking all alone forever with no "be good herself treats". With no one to give them to her. No one to care.

After remembering her manners and introducing herself as Bea the wee bear, the puppy in front of her introduced herself as Bea the homeless puppy. What ? Another Bea ? What would she ever do? There could never be more than one Bea, unless it were the kind that make her "be good to myself" treat. She smiled as she remembered the confusion when her mom would be calling her and the wrong bee would come,. She decided that she would name her Sweet Puppy. Wow, here she was again doing her very familiar TRYING TO FIX THE UNFIXABLE exercise. This problem was much bigger than she could ever fix, even in her greatest IMAGINATION and PRETENDING. She knew she needed to do her talk to THE MAKER OF PUPPIES first. How could she and THE MAKER help this forlorn, nearly hairless, stick-like creature in front of her. She had almost no hair on her hindquarters.

34

Once again, Bea realized she hadn't taken a breath and that she needed to remember to be ALERT but RELAXED. She also had to help Sweet Puppy to find HOPE. So she did her BRAIN exercise said a poem to Sweet Puppy.

You look so sad, I know your life has been so bad

I want to take you home, so you won't be alone

You'll never be so thin, not after I've taken you in

Your name is Bea, so I know you're meant for me

You'll be a happy, happy puppy, and meet my babykitty who was Scruffy

Scruffles, now eats fish, I will make sure to fill your dish

We can all sleep in one big room, far away from any loud boom

Together, we will figure our problems out, if you will just turn yourself about

Will you please come and live with us, I'm sure there will be no big fuss

There was a terrible silence. And then another silence. And then another. Bea wasn't sure she could stand the BUZZING of the fifty bees flying around inside her. The FEAR was bigger than it ever had been. Just as she remembered how THE MAKER had always helped her, a nice comforting HUM filled the air, of busy bees making honey. She knew things would work out for all of them; Scruffles, Sweet Puppy and Bea the wee bear.

Because Bea had, herself, been busy doing her BRAIN exercise, she hadn't been doing her NOTICE exercise. She began to hear a WHINING sound. She wasn't sure if it was a sad WHINING or a happy WHINING. But a skinny wagging tail told her Sweet Puppy was going to say she would be happy to join Scruffles and her.

They could be seen walking toward home, moving side to side as if doing a HAPPY DANCE exercise.

A Terrible Boom

Bea was once again very relieved to learn that puppies don't really like honey, but do like fish; her "be good to myself" treat was safe. For this, she would gladly catch more fish. Just to make sure no FEARS would be growing and there would be enough fish, Bea did her talk to THE MAKER OF FISH exercise.

Bea was surprised how none of them really minded getting wet. Scruffles even played a bit trying to catch some minnows. Sweet Puppy did the "doggy paddle" in shallow water. This made her laugh harder than she had ever laughed before. A real bear belly laugh. Everyone got out and shook the water off as if they were shaking some of their bad memories off.

Sitting comfortably in their comfortable home, Sweet Puppy told both Scruffles and Bea what she was wanting so badly to forget. The man she lived with yelled very loudly and slammed things around. He even made holes in the walls. She tried to distract the man when he went toward the woman by barking at him; but the man took his belt off and scared her so much that she went into her corner. Then the man threw her into a cold room, slammed the door, and left her, where she shook all alone in the dark. She said she did not mind the darkness of the cave because it was different there. No one was going to hurt her and no loud noise.

When Sweet Puppy said the words LOUD NOISE, Bea had a bad memory of when she was very little. She was outside coloring in the sun with her mom. Gradually, her mom began to do her NOTICE exercise as the wind grew stronger. Bea's papers blew away from her purple crayon, as the tree tops were bending more and more toward them. Her mom scooped her up as she lept after her hard work.

Bea was surprised how dark it had become in just those few moments. Her mom set her down as they entered their cave. She dropped her purple crayon, which she had been gripping, when there was a very loud deafening boom. The FEARS started to grow as she remembered the next thing that happened. It didn't seem real now. It couldn't have really happened. But she knew it had, because every time she heard a loud boom she would put her paws up over her head. That's what she wished she'd been able to do as the ceiling of the cave came down on her head with a big branch sticking through an unwelcome big hole. There was more than a honey pot full of dirt covering her as her mom lovingly picked her up, brushed her off, and gave her a big mom bear hug. When they dared go outside, they found a very large elm tree had fallen on the roof of their home.

Ever since that time Bea did not like thunder and lightning storms. And that was what was happening right now. She wished Timothy the Beaver could be there with them. But Beavers don't like caves very much and want to be in the water too much. He often sadly slapped his tail one sound slap as she passed by. But she was still happy to see him and he was happy to see her and she would often find he's left her several new pots; as he knew how often she might drop the empty ones. She did miss him so.

But this was not a time to do the DISTRACTED exercise. Sweet Puppy was beginning to shake more and more. Bea was afraid if she didn't do her ALERT exercise soon Sweet Puppy might have a heart attack. Her FEARS could not get in the way. And she had so many of them. She was conflicted with how to be able to see the lightning and be far enough away from the opening so that Puppy couldn't see it.

For Bea, counting after the lightning helped her to know if the storm was coming closer or going away. She needed to remember how to count the way her mom had taught her. She knew the storm was getting closer if there were fewer numbers in her counting and was relieved when there were more numbers on this count than after the last lightning flash.

Puppy was terrified when she saw lightning because she knew a terrible boom was coming. Bea got Puppy and herself into the farthest corner of the cave. The only problem was that neither of them could know when the next terrible boom was coming. They just sat there clinging to each other. Every once in awhile Puppy just had to peek out of the cave opening to see if there was any lightning; but would run back shaking. Just before she had time to do her talk to the MAKER OF LIGHTNING exercise, there was a loud terrible boom that made the whole cave shake. She had wanted to keep Puppy and herself safe. She had also included Scruffles even though he didn't seem to be phased one bit by any of this. He was actually sitting at the mouth of the cave. It was almost eerie to see his CALM silhouette against the rest of the forest lit up. He definitely was no help. Bea wanted someone to share in the trauma. She guessed it was always going to be just her and Sweet Puppy who would be cowering in the safest darkest corner of the cave.

She sat there shaking, with her "if only's" and "why's" and "no it can't be's". Doing her NOTICE exercise, she realized, she was feeling very young as if the tree had just come down on her cave again. She felt she was right back there again with the dirt covering. Her eyes were so tightly shut that she didn't see that Puppy was struggling against her clutching her so tightl. When she let up on her grip, her thoughts went to her great need for her "be good to myself" treat. If only she could get to it, she have just a little. She was sure it would make everything all better.

Then her DOUBTS came creeping in. She questioned her ability to keep anyone safe. But she knew that even though her FEARS were growing and she wasn't sure she could stand the BUZZING of the fifty bees flying around inside her; she had to do her talk to THE MAKER OF LIGHTNING exercise.

She didn't know if THE MAKER OF THUNDER was the same as THE MAKER OF LIGHTNING but she was pretty sure it was. So she did her talk to THE MAKER OF EVERYTHING exercise. Then after a few quiet minutes, she heard a nice comforting hum in the air, of busy bees making honey and she knew things would be ok.

For some reason, she knew that they could go back outside and maybe even see a rainbow. Scruffles was already sniffing the fresh air and had begun sunning himself to dry off. She did her NOTICE exercise and saw that there was not just one rainbow but a double rainbow with all the colors so clear. After doing her BRAIN exercise, Bea had to admit that THE MAKER OF RAINBOWS would not have been able to put that beautiful gift in the sky, wrapped in a double striped ribbon, without the help of thunder, lightning, rain and most importantly, the SUN.

Bea's Wisdom

One thing Bea the wee bear doesn't have any trouble sharing is the wisdom she has received from the MAKER OF THE BEES. She has found much wisdom in her honey pots during some of her exercises. She had gotten pretty good at doing her BRAIN exercise and FINE MOTOR WEIGHT LIFTING at the same time -- which simply means she could figure things out while enjoying her "be good to myself" treat.

One time when she thought there was no honey left in any of her honey pots, she decided it was time to do her INVESTIGATION exercise. Using her wee nose to look inside each empty pot to see if there might be just enough to do just a few more FINE MOTOR WEIGHT LIFTING exercises; she found that the pots were not empty after all. They were not full of honey; but were filled with something almost better for a wee bear who was doing some BRAIN exercises to figure out whether or not to get involved in someone's problems.

There was all kinds of wisdom to be found while searching each one out. It turned out to be a MEDITATION exercise, where Bea at first thinks of nothing other than the inside of each empty pot. Because there is nothing to distract her except the emptiness of the pot, her mind can be empty. And then become filled with wisdom.

Bea may not always have understood what wisdom means but she surely knows how it has helped to answer many,

many questions. It's a kind of "just knowing something." As she sat doing her BRAIN exercise, she got an idea and then another and another. Each pot, as she stuck her nose into it, became filled with an answer to her question. She was afraid that one particular pot would be filled with her wee bear nose when she got a little too deep in her INVESTIGATION exercise and got her nose stuck. She then had to do her DETACHING FROM THINGS WHICH HAVE A HOLD ON YOU exercise. We have seen that time and time again Bea has struggled to use this wisdom. She can't seem to remember what can happen when someone gets their nose stuck in very uncomfortable places which are not meant for them like a clay pot of honey or in this case -- someone else's business.

Sometime before meeting her dear friend Scruffles the Raccoon Cat. She was feeling very lonely and wanted to understand more about being lonely. She decided to talk to the MAKER OF THE BEES, who knows about how things go when Bea has too much or too little. She realized that being lonely is something like her honey pots when they no longer have any honey left. Yes, that's it; she gets an EMPTY feeling -- a VERY, VERY EMPTY feeling, with a HOLLOW sound echoing all around inside her as if the fifty buzzing bees have left and there is only emptiness.

She stills herself and does her BRAIN exercise and thinks about this getting beyond moments of loneliness is similar to how she might solve her problem when her honey pots are empty. She has done her hungry STROLLING exercise on the way to a friend to ask for more but often she gets to their doors and there's no answer. There are some places where they've said they'd leave the key under the mat for her, but they'd forgotten to leave the key. Some of her friends lived in places fairly inaccessible to Bea. The doors might be too small, too high, or too deep in the ground. And if she did by chance find someone home she unfortunately would have too much difficulty in holding herself back from asking them for all of their honey and instantly wear out her welcome. Somehow she could never bring herself to do things in moderation. Ah, that was just another on her list of exercises she could definitely begin to practice. And if she stopped to consider her friends' needs she would realize she would be leaving them with only empty pots. No one would be any better off. Soon her newly acquired honey would be gone and again she'd be holding only empty honey pots. The other thing she could do is just sit and do nothing and STAY HUNGRY and be MISERABLE.

But the best, the most productive and the most rigorous exercise she could do was to go in search of her favorite honey tree. She realizes only she can solve her loneliness problem. Just like going to search for honey in uncertain places, she needs to find the friend that she knows is really going to be there for her as we have seen proven with her enriching relationships with Timothy and Willow. And of course she knows that her two best cave mates, Scruffles and Sweet Puppy will do the best they can.

She is suggesting for us, this rigorous BRAIN exercise in particular, among all others, because, even though it is very rigorous, it can be most effective in helping us to realize that we are all like her honey pots, sometimes FULL but sometimes EMPTY. Sometimes lonely. Sometimes not. That's just the way of things.

Someone Caring

You are finally going to meet Timothy whom you have heard mentioned in many ways. Just as I was impressed, you will also be very impressed with everything about him. Bea met Timothy on one of her STROLLING exercises. Besides helping her to be wee, we have surely seen how these exercises helped her to find and keep friends, which was so different from when she was younger. These exercises brought her out of her cave, which at times was where she preferred to stay, in her dark, dark empty cave away from everyone, with her sad memories and her "be good to myself" treat. Venturing out, she always came back with a gift, whether it was a new seed to plant in her empty pots, the excitement of a newly discovered spot to do her BRAIN exercises or the nice memory of an encounter with a new friend.

Meeting Timothy was like discovering a very valuable treasure. Every time she spent time with him she felt better and better about herself and her life. She had spent a lot of time worrying about her dear friend Scruffles and Sweet Puppy and helping them. This time it was her turn to have someone care about her and Timothy certainly did show it. When a little voice inside her told that she didn't deserve to have someone care about her, she remembered that time her mom told her that she was a GOOD WEE BEAR. She believed it now, after carrying the question with her for so many years.

Scruffles had taught her that she was a GOOD WEE BEAR by the way he had come to love her over the years, purring so happily around her and sticking by her when she was very sad or scared. She knew that he really cared about her when he didn't run away if she nuzzled her face into his nice soft fur to cry when she was sad. He always seemed to know when she was scared without her having to say; for he stayed by her side, rather than going by himself as independent cats often do.

Sweet Puppy seemed to be much more like Bea. She worried and didn't settle down very easily. She didn't seem to know what to do with or about her bad memories that would come rushing back without warning. Bea was certain that Puppy had nightmares even in the day. She would whine so mornfully in her sleep. Unlike Scruffles who was content to nibble on fish all day, Puppy seemed to want to eat all of the time; a lot like Bea. And the times that immediately come to Bea's memory was every time there were thunder and lightning storms both of them would sit together in the back of the cave with some of the flashes of lightning brightening the walls of their cave. They were no help to each other.

And Puppy was even frightened of lightning bugs ! Bea guessed that Puppy thought they were lightning even though Bea tried to convince her that they were nice little friends and would not hurt us. In fact Bea loved lightning bugs. She loved the way they danced, lighting up the woods. They were so silent, she imagined what music they were making with a light soft rhythmic twinkling sound. She decided that it didn't seem to be the right time to tell Sweet Puppy how delighted she was one time when about five of them entered the cave lighting up the walls in very pretty designs.

She decided the best thing to ever say is that she would keep Puppy safe. In doing her NOTICE exercise, she became aware that she seemed to do more worrying about Scruffles and Sweet Puppy than they did about her. And she hated to admit it to herself, but neither Scruffles nor Puppy were very reliable cuddlers. What a trio; they were all very wounded. She was to be the HEALER. Both Sweet Puppy and Scruffles had already had such terrible lives that Bea tried too darned hard to make things better for them, no matter what it took. Sometimes, she did all the wrong things which made everything get worse; but she did them for the right reasons. Other times, she did do the right things; but they were probably for the wrong reason. She was trying to force a problem to come out the way SHE THOUGHT IT SHOULD -- not the way the MAKER knew would be best. She had changed since meeting Scruffles and Sweet Puppy; but with Timothy now in her life, caring about her, she would find her outlook on things and herself changing even more.

Crashing and Crunching

Often, while rearranging her honey pots, Bea would do her BRAIN exercise. During these quiet moments, she would remember to thank the MAKER OF THE BEAVER, especially talented woodcarving beavers. She believed that the MAKER had Timothy paddle into her life for many wonderful reasons. He was, foremost, a woodcarver. As time passed, he began to carve more and more furniture for her humble cave. The very handsome cupboard which held her most precious honey pots, the very sturdy stepstool that she used for her rigorous exercise program, and the very ornate clay pots were all made by him.

One time, when she was vigorously doing her STEPSTOOLING and WEIGHT LIFTING, the weights got too tippy and went crashing to the floor. She was so upset, she immediately stopped all of her other exercises and began her ON GUARD exercise; her FEARS were back. She didn't exactly understand why she was feeling so unsafe, but had an idea it had to do with when she was little and others used to call her CLUMSY BEAR. Because she was so focused on not being criticized, her FEARS got in the way of her thinking and she forgot to do her NOTICE exercise and stumbled over a root hidden by the thick soft layer of pine needles. Good thing it was a very thick blanket because she landed hard. But what hurt the most was the belittling laughter.

What could she ever tell Timothy? She frantically began her TRYING TO FIX THE UNFIXABLE exercise. She tried to glue and stick the pieces back together with honey. Her "be good to myself" treat had helped with many other problems in the past, but not this time. The jagged pieces would not hold together well enough to look like the clay pot it used to be or to even look like ANY clay pot. She felt like a fragile cracked pot, ready to fall apart and never to be put back together again. She jaggedly remembered that one of the glues of a good friendship is honesty. She did her talk to the MAKER OF TRUTH exercise. After a very quiet moment she was sure she heard the gentle slapping, sounded upon water. She knew somehow things would work out for both of them.

She immediately set off for TIMOTHY'S POND. She found him busily planting some new young trees, which he had started with acorns and seeds from pine cones which she and he had gathered over time. When she cautiously and trustingly told him what had happened he smiled, not a sneer as she was so used to, but a "knowing" smile. Did Timothy have wisdom too? He began to tell her of the many, many, many clay pots he had broken, or a better word would be DEMOLISHED. You see, after he had finished making a nice line of clay pots and had left them to dry in the sun, he decided to cut some trees. You guessed it. And not just one tree came crashing down on the newly dried pots! And not only that time, either.

When others might get very upset about serious things, Timothy the Talented Beaver had such a wonderful way of making them seem almost funny. Bea had never been able to laugh and take things so lightly before meeting Timothy. If there were a way of knowing when a bear smiles you would be able to see the widest and most contented smile on Bea the wee bear's face. She knew that she was certainly smiling in her heart, anyway. Another fact that put her mind at rest was that beavers did not care for honey; their most favorite food was tree bark.

Now, Bea may have snacked on some fine grasses when no honey was available, but never on tree bark. That she could remember. Timothy did not have such an easy time getting at it. The best and most tender bark was at the top of the hardwood trees and since he couldn't climb way up there, he regretfully had to cut down a lot of trees. One of the reasons he made sure to plant some new ones was that he was concerned that someday there wouldn't be any trees left, and he did not want to be responsible for that. Bea had an excellent idea. Maybe by now you have guessed what it was. Beavers can't climb trees, but wee bears can. Timothy thought her idea was excellent too. Now he could go about the job of choosing the right trees to fell for carving and building his dam and canals; and best of all to be able to upgrade his home which he calls a LODGE.

So up the tree Bea went. First, she climbed, only in her mind. She actually had NEVER climbed a tree in reality. She heard bears could do it. So now her pretending and not being absolutely HONEST was giving her some CONSEQUENCES. She wasn't even sure how to start; but with great TREPIDATION, she soundly dug her sharp claws on her hind paws as high up on the tree as she could. Then quickly dug in with her front claws so as not to tip over backwards with no cushioning of comfy pine needles to land in. She talked to THE MAKER all the way up and remembered not to look down at Timothy; even to see if he was smiling, had a worried look in his kind eyes, or trusted her and was going about his scheduled tasks.

She somehow made it to the very top where those tender shoots grow. She broke off as many as she could so she might NEVER have to do that again. As she let them drop one by one, her FEARS started to grow. How would she EVER get back down to the safe ground. Talking to THE MAKER helped her with her BRAIN exercise. Who would ever have thought she'd be doing her BRAIN exercise at the top of a tree! Many claw marks up.

Somehow, she figured out how to go back down one step at a time by thinking backwards. As long as Bea knows what that means; that's all that counts. That was an adventure which she would NEVER forget. Timothy was so pleased and proud of her. That fact almost made it worth it. In addition to learning how to climb up and then climb down a very tall tree, Bea learned several other things:

1. Don't act like you know something, when you don't have any idea what you're talking about at all.
2. Don't offer to do something until you have done your INVESTIGATION exercise.
3. Don't do something if you don't have confidence in yourself for the task, getting very hurt is not going to build your confidence.
4. Do take care of yourself, before you try to take care of someone else.
5. Do remember that when you put yourself in a DANGEROUS situation to kind of rescue a person in their needs, they most probably could and would figure something else out.

At this point Bea was tired of learning and talking about it. She just wanted to forget it all, for awhile and ENJOY HER LIFE. But that always seemed short-lived. Bea did a lot of laughing with Timothy because he told a lot of funny stories about things that had happened to him. But sometimes he seemed to get sad and would tell about something that happened to him when he was younger that was not funny. As they STROLLED down some of the best paths, Bea had begun finding good seeds or little saplings for Timothy to plant. As you may know Beavers favor the hardwood trees. Often they would walk about looking at how the little trees were doing, feeling so good about everything.

On one such occasion, Timothy was quiet for a moment, but then began telling Bea of a time when he was younger and how he had had many, many trees like this, planted on a nice plot of land. He told of how good he felt about himself and his life, unlike his beaver brother, who always seemed unhappy, but never did anything about it. One late afternoon, resting after a very busy beaver day, he heard a very strange sound. When he went to investigate, to his horror, he saw his beaver brother's friend, The Greedy Goat, crunching on his new struggling saplings. His heart sank at the sound and worse yet, his jealous brother was watching the whole time. Pine trees grow very quickly and make a great screen to hide the good trees. But either the goat didn't care or the pine trees just were not able to grow fast enough. Bea loved Timothy even more, now. He also had bad memories. Just like Willow, Scruffles, Sweet Puppy and of course Bea, herself. She hoped so much, that he might often talk to THE MAKER, but of course would never ask. She somehow thought he did talk to the MAKER OF EVERYTHING. She didn't know why, but it just seemed that he did.

Waiting

After spending time with Timothy and his little growing trees, and after doing some BRAIN exercises, Bea has come to look at many things in a different way. When she stays home, she has all kinds of friends come to visit her in all kinds of weather. She always hopes that they are bringing a little of her "be good to myself" treat. This will probably never change. But, on rainy days, besides pots of honey and colorful umbrellas, they bring dark clumps of mud. Bea has heard a lot of complaints and apologies about mud from different creatures.

In one of her BRAIN exercises she got the wisdom to know that the MAKER OF RAIN would not have made mud if it weren't good for something. After all, Timothy uses it to make pots. The nuisance about mud seems to be because it gets on paws or claws, then drops off on different areas of the floor or on furniture. Because mud is damp or wet the complainers have to wait for it to dry and then sweep it up and throw it back outside, only to turn into mud again during the next rainfall, to be tracked in again, to be swept up, to be tracked in again. Bea calls this a SENSELESS exercise. Not an exercise she would want to practice.

She is sure there are better and more sensible things to do with mud than sweep it up and track it in. She has noticed that a lot of the mud comes from the top of the ground, so it must have good topsoil in it. After her generous mud donating friends have left, and she has made sure she has done her FINE MOTOR WEIGHT LIFTING, she gets out her straw broom and wooden dustpan, carved by Timothy. Watching Timothy had given her a great idea. She would plants seeds of all kinds which she had found during her little rigorous STROLLING exercises. And plant them in her empty pots, of which she sadly has many. Empty is never good.

Soon there would be green and colorful things growing all over inside her home. Taking them outside for rain and sun. She is very kind to these plants and places them in the SOUTHERN opening of her cave; for she knows that most plants love the SOUTHERLY EXPOSURE. She also knows that WAITING FOR SEEDS TO GROW is a better exercise than the TIRED WAITING others do when they are WAITING FOR THE MUD TO DRY and thinking terrible thoughts about the mud and whose mud it is and the time they are spending waiting for it to dry.

Waiting for a seed to sprout or a flower to grow doesn't feel like waiting. She thinks this is a good time to busy herself with her "Be wee with Bea" exercises, taking time out, of course for her "be good to myself" treat. Many of these seedlings will be perfect for Timothy too.

A Good Laugh

A new friend who came to visit more and more was a cat that Bea remembered was named Harriet. Bea didn't say anything to Scruffles, but made a plan in her mind, as she was so often to do regarding Scruffles. SCANNING and PLANNING. Her plans, as you may remember, don't always work out the way Bea wants them to, but the way THE MAKER thinks best. Bea was enjoying her special friendship with Timothy and knew how much happier she was now, not that she was unhappy before; but it felt good to be thought of by Timothy as SPECIAL.

She knew that Scruffles certainly was not unhappy, but could always be happier, as any of us could. She encouraged Scruffles to get out more, hoping to herself that he would run into Harriet. She did some of her ON GUARD exercises when she saw them playfully chasing and dancing each other around, making sure that no other creature disturbed them. Bea sometimes would dance a little too. She had become a very practiced dancer. She was so happy when Harriet would come over to visit Scruffles; she would fix them up some "be good to themselves" treat -- fish -- which she caught in her favorite fishing spot.

She got such enjoyment watching them sunning themselves together. She could tell, Scruffles looked forward to seeing Harriet. After a few days had passed and no Harriet, Bea began to worry. As we know she worried about those she cared about. A week later part of the mystery was solved. Harriet must have gotten very injured by a car or other animal. She must not have been able to get to see Scruffles. Harriet must have been nursing her wounded leg; the terrible redness of her flesh was only beginning to heal. Bea wondered also wondered if another bully cat had hurt her the way Orion and Sam had hurt Scruffles, but this looked different. She was so glad that Harriet felt a need to visit Scruffles, in spite of her needing to heal further.

Bea had learned a little from her INVESTIGATION exercises which ended up with her nose in a very sticky situation. But, as you might imagine, not enough -- and she was about to get quite a surprise and have quite a laugh. A bear belly laugh. She had been doing all of the MINDING SOMEONE ELSE'S BUSINESS exercises. But this time, in her head; so she felt this was quite an improvement. But she still was SCANNING and PLANNING. She could stand it no longer. She had to ask Scruffles how things were going between him and Harriet.

When she said "Harriet," he looked very puzzled. Bea told how she had been enjoying watching him and Harriet play together. Having been around Timothy and his laughter, Bea did not feel hurt, but puzzled when Scruffles laughed. She had to laugh at herself too. She was beginning to have a sense of humor for the first time in her whole wee bear life. That was going to become another "Be Wee With Bea" exercise in her program, which had developed into quite a lengthy list. Not taking herself so seriously had given her more opportunity to do her NOTICE exercise. To NOTICE the beauty around her and to NEVER to forget to thank THE MAKER OF EVERYTHING. In answer to her question, he said, "My friend's name is Ozzie, not Harriet". And we will leave it at that, only to take a moment to imagine the lessons Bea could have learned from this incident.

EPILOGUE

As we have seen, Bea the wee bear has found exercises that have helped her to solve problems. Some might say she is a great success and that she must have some magic formula to be able to live as happily as she does, even though things do not always go the way she wishes they would. One very important bit of wisdom she has gotten from the MAKER OF THE MUSTARD SEED, which is so very, very wee, is how to be wee and yet be thought VERY, VERY GREAT by THE MAKER.

You see, she doesn't really very often see life as a problem, as long as she remembers to talk to THE MAKER. We've seen many times when she'd forgotten to do that. But when she finally did her talk to THE MAKER exercise, she calmed down and things worked out as they were supposed to.

We have seen how at first, Bea thought that she needed to fix every problem she saw. But in learning to be wee, she has found a new way to be happy. We are not just talking about her wishing that she had a wee body. No, being wee has come to mean so much more to Bea. Whenever she talks to the MAKER to ask for help in solving big, big problems, she realizes she is wee, and that she cannot make anything go right without the help of the MAKER. Did you notice, she never named herself Bea the Great Bear, not even when she was talking about her paw prints on BEA'S GOLDEN PATH. She did not really understand what the word HUMBLE meant, but the MAKER asked her to do a HUMBLE EXERCISE -- which simply meant that she would take time out of her other exercises to thank the MAKER OF ALL THINGS for any and all of the gifts she has discovered. Especially the music all around her and of course her friends and her ability to breathe when she remembered.

Being wee also meant that she listened to all things, to hear the message the MAKER wanted her to hear. She learned that as long as she remembered to be WEE, she would be GREAT. This sometimes confused her, but she had learned not to question the ways of the MAKER OF ALL THINGS and especially, the MAKER OF WEE BEARS.

I wanted you to meet Bea, to walk along BEA'S GOLDEN PATH, to do some of her rigorous exercises, to discover some of her wisdom, to learn to listen to all the living things around you -- don't forget the rocks -- they just might have something to teach you. But, most of all, I hope that by your meeting Bea the wee bear, you have learned to Be Wee With Bea.

GLOSSARY

BRAIN EXERCISE

Serious thinking and/or meditation

STROLLING

Walking with great alertness

STEPSTOOLING

Going up and down a step stool to get clay pots of honey

FINE MOTOR WEIGHT LIFTING

Using the paw to lift gobs of honey from the pot to the mouth

TOE TOUCHING

Not wanting to waste a drop of honey, bending over to earnestly clean the gooey toes

FLOOR TOUCHING

Similar to toe touching except having to bend over further, to the floor

BULLY

To taunt, call names, belittle by laughing, exclude from activities, emotionally pushy, often resulting in long term trauma and emotional scarring

NOTICE EXERCISE

Really focus on what is in front of you, to really see things as they are, all done without distraction; a good way to clear the mind

PLANNING AND SCANNING

A little bit of plotting to figure out how to solve someone's problem that is basically unsolicited, this often ends up badly

STUCK

Unable to move on; fixated on an idea or situation or problem

FEARS

A form of anxiety, often resulting from trauma from a painful or frightening incident or bullying

TRYING TO FIX THE UNFIXABLE EXERCISE

A form of denial, lack of acceptance of situations as they are

HUMBLE EXERCISE

Very important for progress, needing to think of others rather than just oneself, to be grateful, not unnecessarily self important, yet recognizing and admitting one's own strengths, a balance comes to exist

PRETENDING

Not being totally honest with oneself or others, it is often a learned form of lying and may be unconsciously done, sometimes done to take care of another's feelings

Printed in the United States
By Bookmasters